When I grow up

Andrew Daddo   Jonathan Bentley

ABC
Books

To Whoops and Parps - still growing up - AD
To Mum and Dad, for letting me be me - JB

The ABC 'Wave' device and the 'ABC KIDS'
device are trademarks of the Australian
Broadcasting Corporation and are used under licence
by HarperCollins*Publishers* Australia.

First published in Australia in 2015
by HarperCollins*Children'sBooks*
a division of HarperCollins*Publishers* Australia Pty Limited
ABN 36 009 913 517
harpercollins.com.au

HarperCollins*Publishers*
Level 13, 201 Elizabeth Street, Sydney, NSW 2000, Australia
Unit D1, 63 Apollo Drive, Rosedale, Auckland 0632, New Zealand
A 53, Sector 57, Noida, UP, India
1 London Bridge Street, London SE1 9GF, United Kingdom
2 Bloor Street East, 20th floor, Toronto, Ontario M4W 1A8, Canada
195 Broadway, New York, NY 10007, USA

National Library of Australia Cataloguing-in-Publication data:

When I grow up / Andrew Daddo; Jonathan Bentley, illustrator.
978 0 7333 3341 5 (hardback)
978 1 4607 0281 9 (ebook)
For pre-school age.
Dreams – Juvenile fiction.
Imagination – Juvenile fiction.
Picture books.
Bentley, Jonathan, illustrator.
A823.4

The illustrations in the book were created using charcoal pencil and watercolours
Cover and internal design by Jonathan Bentley and Darren Holt, HarperCollins Design Studio
Colour reproduction by Graphic Print Group, Adelaide
Printed and bound in China by RR Donnelley on 128gsm Matt Art

7 6 5   16 17 18 19

When I grow up, I'd like to be the school principal.

school principal

What do you
want to be?

I want to be a hairdresser!

Taming goldy locks will be my thing.

Imagine the buns and the braids ...
the bobs and the beehives!
The boys will have buzzcuts or bowls.

So much hair,

so many stories ...

Well, when I grow up, I want to be an inventor.
I could create a whizz-bang new rocketship!

inventor

A bowl that never runs out of lollies!

And imagine a supersonic skateboard with no speed wobbles!

a **tallness** machine!

A table clearer ...
a dishwasher stacker and unstackerer ...

a bedroom cleaner

(that's not called me!).

And for my greatest invention of all ...

I'll invent an invention inventer!

There's only one place I want to work – and it's up there.
I'm going to be an astronaut!

I could even use that whizz-bang rocketship.

I'll float in space from sun up to sun up —
'cause the sun's always up in space.

There'll be things to fix, stars to see

and worlds to photograph.

It's going to be ASTRONOMICAL!

I want to tell stories so **big** they'll have to **stuff** them into books!

Epic adventures about pirates with black teeth and pegs for legs ...

I see goblins and dragons,
and lots of smoke and fire.

A magician will make things disappear,
and only I'll know
where to find them.

A prince will rescue
a princess, and she'll say,

'I can rescue myself,
thank you!'

The Greatest Book Ever
by Me

But they'll still live
happily ever after ...

Shhh ... I'm in training to become a secret agent ...

I'll have disguises and bulletproof hair.
You won't even know I'm me.

My mum won't even know what I do.

So don't tell anyone –

or I'll have to silence you.

Can you hear it? That's the stage calling me ...
I'm going to be a performer!

performer

When those bright lights hit me, there'll be *drama* and *singing* too.
But best of all will be the moves I groove ...

Watch me twirl ...

watch me swirl ...

see me tap ...

see me flap ...

watch me krump ...

watch me jump.

See my feet find the beat!

My mum says I could be lots of things ...

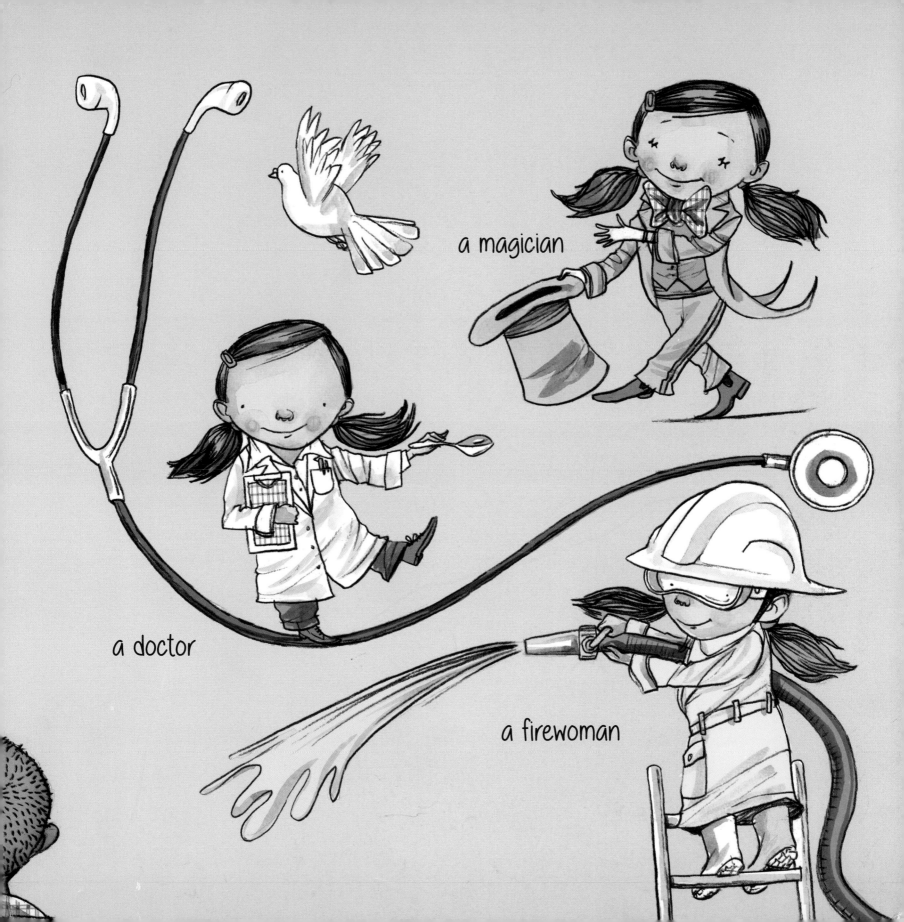

a magician

a doctor

a firewoman

a chef

a tennis player

a vet